Love
without
FEAR

Cassi, & family

May God Bless You + Your family

Love,
Shameka

5/14/2018

Shameka Walker

www.askshameka.com

(678) 628-8398

Family Secrets

Innocent, young, pure, full of energy was she,
Until a loved one stole her virginity.
Lost, not knowing to turn left or right;
The sound of a familiar voice far out of sight,
Suddenly, no one understands or cares to hear,
Please MOM! Please DAD! Lend me a moment of your ear!
Lonely, scared, no one to turn to;
Weird one moment; happy the next: blue.
Dreams destroyed, hopes left unexplained;
Quietly she asked for a one-way ticket from Mississippi to Maine.
Once again a word from that familiar voice,
"Stay, don't run - the pain and suffering was not your choice."
Thinking of college, work, a new beginning; quickly she left,
No one will ever know that behind the smile lies the truth
of how she felt.
The girl filled with joys, hopes, and dreams;
Sometimes proves things are not always what they seem
Eager to explain, no one could see;
So she hid the hurt from her family.
Unaware that it wasn't her fault,
She decides to run; FREE! No man was caught.
Parents too busy; so little time,
Failed to realize there was a crime,
So traumatic within their home,
That their little girl was feeling alone.
Male loved one has no heart, no fear, lack of understanding;
Destroyed faith, love, the beginning
Didn't give her a chance
To let her beauty enhance
He hides behind what no man knows,
Blood is thicker than water as it shows.

Shameka Jenette Walker

A Dedication to My Sisters

This book is dedicated to my sisters who have been sexually, mentally, emotionally, physically and spiritually abused while searching for love. It does not matter who hurt you or even why the abuse happened, but it is important that you do not lose yourself in the midst of the pain. Do not allow past hurts and pains to deny you a successful and beautiful future.

It is imperative that you stop, look in the mirror, look yourself in the eyes and say, "I am somebody and I deserve the best life has to offer!" You must love yourself before anyone else can love you. That means feeling comfortable within your own skin.

An essential part of overcoming your past is taking control of your life and destiny. Taking control includes forgiving those who caused you heartache and loving them unconditionally. Sometimes, it is up to you, the victim, to hold your head up, fight your ego and go to your abuser and tell him, "I forgive you for every pain you caused my heart to endure."

I am the first to say it is not easy to forgive. But a large burden was lifted from my inner spirit when I forgave those who mistreated me. Life is too short for you to hold grudges while your abuser receives all the joy. Stop crying late at night, wipe away your tears, swallow your pride, make a stand, take life by the hand, rise up and prove to yourself that You Are Somebody!

After being hurt by those who tell you over and over they love you can cause you to lose your way and even put a barrier between you and true love. Don't push away, judge, or make every man suffer because you have not learned to embrace love. You are going to make mistakes because you are a creature of habit, as am I. You are going to make mistakes because you are a creature of habit, as I am, in our quest for perfect love. But we can learn from our mistakes and turn a negative situation into a positive learning experience. As we learn, we must always remember:

"There is no fear in love; but perfect love casteth out fear: because fear hath torment. He that feareth is not made perfect in love." – (1 John 4:18)

Life is filled with many challenges and endless opportunities. It's up to you as an individual to come to the realization that you must make a change in order to get different results. I am not asking you to forget the past hurts, pains and joys but to simply move forward into your destiny. Sometime we are our own worst enemies and we allow self to hinder us from reaching our fullest potential.

I learned to seek God for understanding. I literally had to fall down on my knees and pray for God to take total control of my life. Even though I knew right from wrong my inner man did not want me to be successful in loving myself first. Neither did he want me to learn what my purpose was as a child of God. I searched for love through the valley, over the hill, and even around the mountain when God just wanted me to let go and let Him drive for a while. Don't get me wrong, I enjoyed the ride but I took the long route to finding love. Just when I ran out of gas God sent my soul mate to rescue me.

Just as the sisters you are going to read about, know who you are as an individual. Learn something from every relationship. Let the negative aspects of your past make you stronger while the positive defines you and encourages you to never give up on your dream of finding true love. Before you can find love you must put God first, forgive freely, and love unconditionally because the devil meant your abuse for your bad but God turned it around for your good.

I cried and prayed many nights often promising God that I would do this, that or the other if he would just take the pain away. Nothing happened until I gave God my heart, body, mind, and soul. Did I break my promises? Yes, without a doubt, and I paid the price for my sins but I never forgot the sweet feeling of peace the moment I cast all my burdens on him.

Just in case you don't know him, let me introduce you to a man named Jesus. The bible says in Philippians 4:13 (KJV) "I can do all things through Christ who strengthens me" and in Jeremiah 29:11 (NKJV) "For I know the plans that I have for you, declares the Lord, plans to prosper you and not to harm you, plans to give you hope and a future." It is God's plan for you to walk in your purpose and live a successful life. There will be days that are worse than others. However, surrounding yourself with positive people who inspire and motivate you to work will help you move to the next level.

My advice to you is to develop an honest relationship with God, study your word daily, join a church family, stay faithful and true to God, and walk in your purpose as a child of God. Be encouraged to take it one day at a time and allow God to use you for his glory only!

Until we meet again,

My Love and My Wife

Over a decade ago I met my beautiful wife and from what I have experienced she have truly demonstrated what it means to "LOVE WITHOUT FEAR." Despite only knowing each other for a few weeks we got engaged, and shortly after we were joined together in holy matrimony. Normally this kind of marriage is what some call short fuse which typically does not last long. But we are the exception to the rule. We have made it this far with the help of God and great communication.

Throughout her life Shameka has dedicated herself to loving and caring for others often time those she cares for hurt her, but that did not stop or slow her down. As often as she is knocked down normally by the same people, she picks herself up, dusts herself off, and love again. She have been living Christ like love. Shameka is an overcomer, an inspiration to many, talented in many ways—a super daughter, sister, aunt, mom, friend, First Lady, and an extraordinary wife.

With such a person like Shameka Jenette Walker I am glad that she is my wife and my partner in ministry. Recently we started a ministry in Canton, Georgia and Shameka have been a pillar of strength. Without her I don't know how I would make it sometime because she keeps me grounded and focus. Without her some of the things I have achieved today would not be possible. Outside of God she is the next best thing. I may be the head, but she is my neck. She is my love and my wife. Thank you baby for being there for me and I wish the very best on your book. I believe it will be on the best seller list soon. You are my love and my wife.

Love Your Husband,

Pastor Samuel H. Walker

Foreword

Love Without Fear, the title itself speaks volumes. This book provides a balanced view of the various elements and complexities that consist within love. This inspiring writing gives definition to many of the situational events that exist within the life of individuals from varied backgrounds.

This book has been penned with the reader in mind by addressing subject matter that may not be confronted in a conventional setting. *Love Without Fear*, takes into account, the diversified meanings and areas that are explored in relationships. The author, Shameka J. Walker, chose a creative and scholarly approach to give the reader an unbiased illustration by using short stories and poetic expressions.

Love Without Fear, provides the realistic outlook of what is a daily occurrence in the lives of many and examines the intricate details; opening the inner story that is the root of the actions and decisions in love and relationships, in general.

As you read this exceptional piece of writing, allow the words to cause all fear to be removed and embrace love in its true form.

Dr. Mia G. McGee
Educator/Entrepreneur
AHP Consulting
www.miamcgee.org

Love

without

FEAR

"By night on my bed I sought him whom my soul loveth: I sought him, but

I found him not."

Song of Solomon 3:1

Chapter One

My First Love: Featuring Pauline

"Quickly and with passion, they embraced. Their lips touched and their desire grew as they held tightly on to each other."

PAULINE HAD TAKEN ALL SHE COULD from her family. Her faith was lost and she wanted to die. What she did not know is that death is not a way out. It could not give her the peace for which she longed.

In misery, she sat in her room pondering the countless problems plaguing her world. Frustrated that the ringing telephone jarred her from her thoughts Pauline considered letting it ring until the caller grew tired of waiting. Her politeness led her to answer as she was the only person home. To her surprise and utter delight, the sweet voice of a gentle angel beamed through the receiver. He asked for someone else only to find Pauline.

What, under normal circumstances, would have been a *sorry for the ring* conversation turned into a lifetime of conversations. Pauline's glum filled night had been interrupted by something wonderful: a spark between her and her new, gentle angel. They began to travel the road of discovery together; moment by moment. Every night the two spoke quietly on the telephone. They asked each other questions and listened with deep concentration to the answers. At times, finding a nice quiet place to hold conversations with the gentle angel was difficult but he was worth every effort.

Pauline and her gentle angel's intense conversations revealed they had a lot in common. So much so, that it became essential for them to meet face to face. Neither one knew what would come of their chance meeting but hope and sweet expectations rested in Pauline's heart. In a few days she would see the gentle angel who had completely turned her life around. She no longer worried about her problems.

It was a glorious sunny day in April when they first laid eyes on each other. Instantly, a wide and wonderful smile gleamed on Pauline's beautiful face. She knew this was the start of a powerful love. Her heart told her it was love at first sight. The gentle angel was mesmerized as he looked deep into Pauline's eyes and confessed to her for the first time that he had fallen in love. Nothing else mattered at that moment; they were finally together.

A solitary tear streaked down Pauline's face. This was not one of the sorrowful tears which had haunted her as she sat alone in her room. This was a tear of joy, shed for their new beginning and true love. The lone tear never traveled the course of the others; the gentle angel caught it in his hand and placed it tenderly over his heart.

"Cry no more. I am here to replace your tears with endless laughter, romance, friendship, hope, faith and love," Pauline's gentle angel explained as he stared into her eyes, his hand over his heart.

Those beautiful words seemed to shake Pauline to her very core. Quickly and with passion, they embraced. Their lips touched and their desire grew as they held each other tightly. Soon, they became lost in heated passion followed by burning lovemaking. Pauline's body responded to his every loving touch. They rolled and rolled under the sheets until they were soaked from a river of love.

Their lovemaking continued until they were completely fulfilled. Exhausted, Pauline slowly fell away from her lover's chest. Looking down at her with a question in his eyes, Pauline gazed up into her angel's eyes, and answered, "I love you too."

Their love was sure and sound but neither was willing to accept the reality that their love was forbidden. Complications existed. They were often mistaken as father and daughter and her gentle angel was loved by another.

Careful to keep their love a secret they spent five days a week together for the next three years. He loved her, took care of her and provided everything she could possibly need. Pauline lovingly, willingly gave herself—mind, soul and body. The two shared a friendship many people envied. As Pauline grew and matured in life she was no longer willing to be second best in her gentle angel's life even though he treated her as his Nubian queen. He gave Pauline his soul but it was not enough to satisfy her every want and need. The overwhelming desire to have the very air he breathed caused Pauline to demand more from her angel. She needed him to survive.

Feeling that he was losing Pauline's undivided attention he lost focus of his own problems and current situation. He began to sacrifice his life, career and family in order to be Pauline's reason for living.

But Pauline had other plans and goals that her angel did not know of—plans to right the wrongs in her life. Her convictions caused her heart to hurt. Every night, she prayed for her angel to fall in love with the one he was with so that she could be free. While their bond was undeniable, Pauline knew that her heavenly Father was displeased with her relationship. Her Gentle Angel didn't want to believe she could exist without his love and that knowledge gave Pauline the energy she needed to emancipate herself from his fantasy world.

Innocent by age and mature by experience, Pauline left for college. Her angel felt betrayed by the distance and made his self unavailable for an excruciating five years. After enduring five years of pure agony not knowing if Pauline was safe, their paths crossed in the same location where they first fell in love.

He glanced into her eyes and became overpowered by the same love that had kept him alive for the past five years. Pauline still craved his unconditional love but was fully aware that their love had run its course. Yet he vowed to never let their love die no matter what path they traveled separately.

Fifteen beautiful years of their undying love had made it possible to overcome any obstacles in life or family.

Chapter Two

My Coach: Featuring Simone

"Simone ran as fast as she could. Her plan was to run straight into the

coach's arms immediately after the grueling practice."

SIMONE ARRIVED AT THE GYM immediately after school already dressed for cross country practice. An exceptional athlete, Simone was excited about the upcoming State meet where she was scheduled to run. She was also exhilarated about her coach pushing her to run a little faster. But most of all, Simone was thrilled about the passionate embraces, the shared love and so much more awaiting her at the end of practice with her coach. Simone ran as fast as she could. Her plan was to run straight into the coach's arms immediately after the grueling practice.

Earlier in the season daily practices would last forever. The only way to keep the practices at bearable lengths, Simone volunteered to become team leader. She did not want a delay in the rendezvous with her love. While thoughts of her coach ran through her head, Simone cheered her teammates on as she easily ran by them, "We can do it team!"

Her goal then was to keep practice short. This particular day was no different. When practice was over, Simone rested longer than necessary to assure she'd be the last girl to leave the gym. A quick look around the locker room confirmed everyone was gone, and with barely concealed excitement she quickly slipped into the back of the boy's locker room. There she found her knight. He was a welcomed sight he stood with his arms outstretched for Simone. She jumped into his arms and whispered softly in his ears with promise, "I have been waiting to feel you inside me all day."

Eager to meet the other's needs, Simone and the coach wasted no time ripping every piece of clothing off their sweaty bodies. As they embraced, the girls' softball coach entered the same locker room to wash uniforms from the earlier game. Only twenty feet away from the washroom, they were forced to keep quiet. Neither one wanted to stop, so they continued to lose themselves in each other, quietly. The excitement of their silent lovemaking caused rushes of adrenaline in them both.

The passion of Simone and her coach surpassed all other concerns. With child-like abandonment, they pretended that no one was there and worked to help each other climax. Simone knew that if she made a sound, her athletic career was over. He knew that his coaching career and freedom were in jeopardy but his love for Simone was all that mattered at that moment.

While the other coach completed her cleaning task, the lovebirds made sexually charged history.

Simone, held from behind by her knight, began to pray to God to never let the moment end. Even though the pressure was high they were able to escape without confrontation but only after they climaxed for the tenth time. Before they left one another they sealed the night and their love with one final sweet kiss.

As graduation was only seven months away, Simone knew that she would miss her coach deeply when their sexcapades ended. With a burning desire to take their adventurous relationship to the next stage her heart was completely aware that her coach was only in her life for a season. Daily, she found herself in a trance fighting the urge to stay or let go of the one person that made her heart skip beats.

Without the strength to let go of such a unique and magical love affair Simone trusted time to make everything wrong right. As the months passed, the coach became distant and unsettle about the overwhelming bond he shared with Simone. Even though he held the upper hand and total control of the situation not even his heart could turn its back on love. After several unanswered phone calls and limited eye contact, Simone came to the realization that if the man she once called her knight walked away, then he would forever carry the burden of wondering, "What if?"

Simone, fighting to gain internal peace, saw his decision as her time to break free. As she prepared for her graduation she looked deeply in her bedroom mirror to encourage herself to be strong for them both. She became over powered by such emotions that she began to pray and ask God to guide her journey in doing the right thing.

As a leader in her class she was the first to enter the stadium for the graduation ceremony. Immediately, her eyes scanned the stadium in search of her coach. Unable to locate him made her heart sad. She had written the graduation speech as a tribute to him. When her name was called to greet the audience she discovered that her coach was standing at the edge of the stadium where they first laid eyes on each other. She smiled a beautiful, satisfied smile. Simone delivered the most motivating and captivating speech; the audience was enthralled. As she took her seat Simone gazed into the coach's deep, smoldering eyes. Her expression said it all. "You will deeply be missed but loved for a lifetime."

Now is the Time

Now is the time, better than never,

Overcome the pain of your past

stormy weather.

With God as your guide you cannot fail.

Ignore God and inherit a ticket from family and

friends to Hell.

Stay focused, faithful,

and true to what you believe.

There will be trials and tribulations,

but your goals you will achieve.

Happiness is knocking at your door

very fast,

Everyday with Jesus

brings joy made to last.

Take a stand and be an example for

others you know,

You won't regret the decision

and in Jesus you will grow.

Many are called but

few are chosen by God,

Either young or old, you must finish the race and

overcome all odds.

Stop Running

Stop running when things

don't go your way,

Wait and listen to what that person

has to say.

Stop running when your child asks

for more time,

It could be a signal or warning sign.

Stop running when the love of your life

decides they're leaving,

Maybe you are being set free

from a heart of bleeding.

Stop running from your past

life of pain,

Because you have no control over

when it rains.

Stop running from what your future holds,

Keep on living and the truth

will be told.

Shameka J. Walker

Chapter Three

My Marine: Featuring Whitney

"Whitney closed the door to her apartment, turned to the room and thought over the previous time she'd spent with The Marine. "He is the one. My search is over," thought Whitney."

WHITNEY HAD FIVE MINUTES before she had to go on stage and model a beautiful blue gown at the fundraiser fashion show. She was shocked because she had been asked to participate in a fashion show as a petite model when she did not consider herself to be petite. Nonetheless, willing to do whatever needed to be done, she agreed to a stroll down the runway.

While there, she met a woman who surprised her by making a surprising declaration to her, "My son is going to marry you." Whitney looked up at the woman, smiled, and politely but firmly responded, "I am already taken." Unaware that she was being watched she went on stage and stole the show.

A few weeks later Whitney received a telephone call from Maryland. Excitement in his voice was unmistakable for he had finally reached the woman of his dreams after many attempts. He noticed the curiosity in her voice when she answered but he was not about to let her go. The stranger was determined to connect with Whitney.

Although Whitney did not know the stranger, she was single and decided not to hang up the phone. One never knew where true love would come from.

The first words from the stranger were a confession that he had unashamedly watched her for over two years. He would have approached her but he was intimidated by her beauty. Though he considered himself to be pretty good looking, Whitney was a woman of such mesmerizing beauty she was completely out of his league.

Whitney loved the great conversation they shared and chemistry began to develop. It was time to take the second step. With only a few weeks before the end of military boot camp they made arrangement to meet. He was nervous because he was overwhelmed about the opportunity to date Whitney, the most popular girl in town.

At last, boot camp was over. Whitney and The Marine were now able to look into each other's eyes to see if there was a connection. To their surprise and delight, not only was there a connection but they couldn't keep their hands off each other.

It was their second date and The Marine arrived at Whitney's house with anticipation. Anxious to share his heart with his dream girl, he drove them as fast as he could to a quiet place. When they arrived he turned to Whitney gently held her hands in his and confessed that she was the girl he dreamed of marrying as a child. After sharing many confidences and many special touches, The Marine whispered in Whitney's ear, "Let's wait until marriage." Breathlessly Whitney exclaimed, "I need you now!" Unable to resist the look in her eyes he threw her down on the bed and began to kiss her from head to toe. He was careful not to miss any inch of her luscious body.

"You have a fine body, my marine. I love the touch of your bulging arms around me. Hold me tight and make sweet, slow love to me. Don't rush sweetheart." The Marine responded by wrapping his arms tightly around her. Amateurs embark on what would have been mastered by pros. They both were surprised by the strong, uninhibited love they offered to one another. Their breathing became labored as they sought to know each other better.

It was getting late and time for The Marine to take Whitney home. He kissed her on the forehead and said good night. Whitney closed the door to her apartment, turned to the room and thought over the previous time she'd spent with The Marine. "He is the one. My search is over," thought Whitney. She had no idea that time would challenge their passion for one another. Even though he worshipped the very ground Whitney walked on, her independency and ambitious goals terrified him. He wasn't sure about making her his wife if he wasn't needed by her. And the one thing he had always wanted; he wanted to be needed by his wife. He longed daily for her intimacy but was intimidated by Whitney's ability to demand attention when she entered a room. He even failed to understand why her eyes revealed a deep driving force for success.

For the next year Whitney listened to him continually confess his love for her but was stunned when he married someone else. He was unable to comprehend Whitney's ability to accomplish every goal she set out to achieve. Whitney's love for The Marine helped her to accept his decision to satisfy his personal ego for what he thought it meant to be a man. Love was not enough of an incentive for Whitney to change her career, become a housewife or lose herself as an individual.

On a cold November night as she held his hand, she set his spirit free. She pushed aside her own needs and informed him that she had accepted his decision to love someone else. Whitney wanted him to love without the fear of losing a dear friend. Therefore, Whitney shared her virtuous personality with the man she thought she would love for a lifetime. Whitney stared into his eyes and told her marine, "I forgive you for every pain you caused me and I love you enough to let you go!"

Chapter Four

My Preacher: Featuring Rachel

"Feeling like a princess she smiled and said, "Thank you. What's on the menu?" The preacher's answer held an undertone of promise, "It is the chef's specialty so just enjoy."

WHILE A FRESHMAN IN COLLEGE, Rachel sought a church home. After prayerfully and carefully searching the phone book and asking others in the area she finally located a place to worship. She felt almost complete because Rachel found comfort she so desperately needed at the church.

Now that she had a church home, she worried about how she would get there every Sunday. She began to pray and ask God for transportation. God heard her prayers and after church one Sunday, the pastor asked his associate elder to provide her with a ride to her dorm. The elder gladly agreed to take her home and they left the morning service after benediction had been said.

On the way to the dorm, they talked about their pasts and how they got involved in the church. Rachel and the associate elder both had interesting backgrounds. Before Rachel got out of his car, he asked for her telephone and dorm numbers. Even though Rachel felt a little unsure she gave him her information. He wasted no time and called her later that night. That was the first of many calls. Although they had busy schedules they still found time to call each other every day. Rachel had a strange feeling she was treading dangerous water but could not resist his charm. He was tall, well-dressed, owned a nice car, and was financially stable. Most of all, he had a strong relationship with God. Rachel knew he was already accounted for but without legal papers. She felt confused but continued to answer all of his calls. Eventually, she accepted an invitation to have dinner at his place.

It was a Monday night when she rode the school's transportation from her dorm to his on-campus apartment. When she arrived at his building, the front desk receptionist recorded her visit. She thought *this is crazy* and started to walk away. Then she heard his voice over the intercom, "Send Rachel right up."

"Thank you," she said to the receptionist before walking straight through the double glass doors to find his room. She could smell the aroma from the food he was preparing before she made it down the hall. The sound of soft music led Rachel to his door. There was no need for her to knock, the preacher opened the door, grabbed her hand and said "welcome to my home." His voice was warm and inviting.

Despite being in a stranger's apartment, Rachel was able get comfortable in the preacher's place. He sat her at his beautifully decorated table that had two plates, two forks, two glasses, two candles and two chairs. Feeling like a princess she smiled. "Thank you. What's on the menu?"

The preacher's answer held an undertone of promise, "It is the chef's special so just enjoy."

After he blessed the food, they ate the delicious feast while taking pleasure in each other's company. Rachel could feel him making love to her with his eyes. In a valiant effort to remain calm and in control of herself, she offered to wash the dishes once they finished their meal. The preacher, aware of Rachel's intentions, was quick to respond. Tenderly but firmly, he replied, "This night is about you. The dishes can wait."

Rachel shivered excitement and anticipation.

The preacher offered her a shoulder massage to relax her body and mind. Feeling a little tense and uptight, she agreed and laid down on the bed. As his large hands moved slowly under her clothing to caress her body she allowed her mind to run free. Before she could come back to reality, she found herself naked and in need of him to go as far as his heart desired. His status in the church had no significance at that moment because they were equally yoked.

As he entered Rachel from behind she began to move away but his large hands held her shoulders in place, allowing no room for movement. The sensation was so passionate they began to convince one another they needed each other. And although they knew they were on the path to spiritual destruction, they refused to stop but worked to satisfy each and every need. With their hands on the floor but their bodies on the bed, they exploded together.

After an hour of deeply, satisfying love-making, they had extra time to evaluate what had just happened and come to a conclusion. The preacher held Rachel against the wall, softly kissed her neck and whispered closely in her ear, "You are worth my soul going to hell!"

Shortly afterward, Rachel left sexually pleased but with a tormented spirit. *How could something that felt so good be so wrong for my mind, body and soul,* she asked herself. For the next week Rachel had a difficult time sleeping and decided to give the preacher a call. Expecting gentleness and encouragement she was faced with the reality that the preacher would never be her everything. This heavy burden of rejection broke her spirit and she began to cry.

As her heart continued to ache, Rachel longed for solace and support. Her mind ran to the only place she found comfort, the church. When she walked through the church that Friday night, the pastor and members were already engaged in prayer. Without delay, Rachel— spiritually and emotionally bruised—threw herself on the altar.

Rachel was determined to get her break through before she left the altar. That night of prayer changed her whole life and outlined her new spiritual walk. She was able to leave church with inner peace although fretful that she would still have to face the preacher. She was deeply bothered about how she would worship freely knowing that she had crossed the line with a very anointed man.

One day after church the preacher confronted Rachel. He longed to know why she was avoiding him in and out of church. At first Rachel found it very difficult to speak her mind but eventually spoke, "Be true to your calling!"

Dismayed, he was unable to speak a single word. Never had anyone resisted his charm nor had the nerve to put him in his place. Those short but powerful words were enough for the preacher to open his closed eyes to his own spiritual walk. Later that night he called Rachel and said, "Thank you for being strong and building enough confidence in yourself to not allow me to misuse my authority for self gratification."

Together they decided not to let their experience hinder their spiritual walk but be an example for others. While working closely with the pastor, they were able to help the church youth department grow from ten members to well over fifty.

Their love for God helped them to overcome the power of sin. Through their ministry many lives were changed and God was able to position them as great leaders in the church, at school, and within the community. It was only after they sinned no more that God was able to use them completely. God awarded their obedience and faithfulness by opening doors that helped them find their soul mates that showered them with true happiness and unconditional love.

I'm grateful

Thank you Lord for another day.

To tell those that I love what I have to say

Grandma, thank you for your wisdom, strength,

and understanding ways.

Grandpa, thank you for your hugs, kisses, and encouragement

to reach for the stars.

Mom, I'm grateful for your support and unconditional love.

Dad, I'm grateful for all your teaching, power, and principles.

My beautiful wife, you are my better half that completes me

and births my visions of life.

My loving husband, you will always be the one that captured my heart

and continues to be my best friend.

My darling daughter, I cherish the day you made me a parent and

I will forever live through your dreams.

My handsome son, you will always have my undivided attention

and turn my frowns into smiles.

Sister, you will forever be a star in my eyes

and a friend to the end.

Brother, your over-protection made me strong

and respect myself as a child of God.

Thank you Lord for another day,

To tell those I love what I have to say.

Grandma, I Appreciate You.

Love Without Fear

Grandpa, I Respect You.

Mom, I Cherish You.

Dad, I Honor You.

Wife, I Admire You.

Husband, I Depend on You.

Daughter, I Believe in You.

Son, I Support You.

Sister, I Look up to You.

Brother, I Trust You.

And to everyone, I Love You.

Thank you Lord for another day.

To tell those I love what I have to say!

Shameka J. Walker

Chapter 5

My Muslim: Featuring Ariel

"Ariel knew that dating outside her faith was a risk but never did she expect to ride the roller coaster of love she experienced with him."

ARIEL HAD BEEN IN FLORIDA SINCE DECEMBER on an assignment for the university where she was employed. Her job required that she travel throughout the State to promote the University to various high school students. She honestly enjoyed sharing her college experience with other teenagers because she had sat in their seats just eighteen months earlier.

Although she was having a great time in Florida her heart was in Rhode Island. She had left her live-in lover in Rhode Island to handle the bills while she was away on business. She missed him terribly.

To help ease the longing for her lover, Ariel spoke with him every night on the telephone until she was too sleepy to continue. They spoke of special and loving things. The times they'd spent together had begun to fill the emptiness in Ariel's heart and she wanted to continue to have the sense of fulfillment her lover brought her. But, just like rain brings nourishment to the earth, it can also create a flood. A gushing of uncertainties troubled her. One of her concerns was that this was her first time loving someone outside her faith. She knew that dating someone with different beliefs was a risk but she never expected to ride the roller coaster of love she experienced with him. It was not her intention to fall for him but when she was away from her lover she missed the good times they shared. Another concern was the regular beating he gave her. The same hands that caressed her would, for no particular reason, strike her. Daily, Ariel asked, "Why do I love this man so much?"

Ariel daily lived her life trapped between the door of heaven and hell. Without a doubt, she knew she needed this time in Florida to evaluate her living arrangements in Rhode Island. But at the same time she did not want to give up on what she thought was an almost perfect relationship.

Her time in Florida would soon end. With that fact in mind, she phoned her lover to invite him to join her for the last week in her apartment, which happened to be during Spring break. He gladly accepted the invitation and booked his flight the same night.

Ariel didn't know how much of a spell her lover had on her until he arrived. Standing 6'3" with a *to-die-for* athletic build, Ariel lost all control when she saw him. She leaped into his arms and kissed him from the baggage claim to the parking lot. Her Muslim gently sat her down at her car. While he stared at her hungrily, she undressed him slowly with her eyes. Ariel had prepared herself mentally and emotionally for whatever the night had in store.

Once they arrived at her apartment they wasted no time getting reacquainted. The sky was the limit as they began the love ritual with which Ariel was familiar. As they leaped to higher heights and deeper depths the bed felt like it was on fire with great flames at all four corners. They didn't care that their bed was in hell as they decided to take their love roller coaster to the next level.

In the midst of having a good time he whispered in Ariel's ear, "I am going to be your daddy tonight."

In the sexiest voice possible, she responded, "Have your way with me Daddy."

They carried on in danger mode as a rapist might with his innocent victim. Neighbors, alarmed at the sounds emanating from the apartment, called the police.

Two hours later they were awakened by a loud knock on the door. "Police. Open up!" said the voices on the other side of the door. Ariel grabbed her clothing and ran to the door as fast as she could. But her lover never made a move or showed an inkling of fear.

Ariel opened the door and found herself face to face with the local police. Following an intensive search of the apartment, the police inquired whether or not anyone had been engaged in sexual activity within the last four hours. Ariel, with the largest, satisfied smile on her face said, "Yes, and we were role playing." The officers laughed, requested that they keep it down a little, and told them to enjoy the rest of their time in Florida.

Knowing that they had just escaped a ticket from hell to jail the lovers pulled all their bedding to the middle of the apartment. Ariel looked into her lover's eyes, became trapped by another spell, and screamed at the top of her lungs, "Was it good to you, Daddy?"

After a week of beautiful fun filled nights, Ariel and her lover returned to Rhode Island. Thinking their time away from each other and the week of romance in Florida had brought them closer, made Ariel feel their relationship still had hope. Unfortunately, her return home was greeted by beatings with the hands that promised to protect and nourish.

The man had such an incredible personality, but no idea how to love an independent, outgoing and educated woman. Ariel had no desire to lower her standards or give up her sanity to conquer love and to be loved. She longed to keep him but not if she had to sacrifice inner peace and outer beauty. Her lover was so good at expressing how he felt. While confronting her after a beating he said, "If I didn't love you I wouldn't beat you. This is how I prove my love."

Ariel looked him straight in his eyes while biting her bottom lip without being concerned about getting hit, opened her mouth and yelled, "You do not love me or you would not continue to hit me!"

That night Ariel searched deep within to regain self respect and self esteem. She made the decision to not allow anyone to tear her down to the point of no psychological return. Even though she never denied that she loved this man, neither could she continue for another three years to be abused for the sake of love. She yearned for answers and the strength needed to walk away. Ariel realized that she had no choice but to remove herself from her comfort zone before this man lead her to an early death.

Later that night as he slept Ariel prayed silently. She asked God to guide and give her the right direction to travel. She was adamant about doing the right thing to decrease the gap between herself and her jealous God. She was at a point of emotional destruction that only God could reach down and pull her up again. With tears running down her face she smiled, opened her eyes, looked up above as saying, "Thank you for a second chance."

Three months passed and the beating didn't stop but Ariel continued to trust God. She started a new job that gave her financial freedom. With her finances in place she gained the confidence she once lacked. She realized that the reason she stayed and endured the beatings were due to the fear of being alone and the lack of financial security. Ariel felt so close to her lover but yet they were so far away from what each of them needed for survival.

It was a Monday morning when Ariel's boss called her into his office. Unsure what was to be expected, she took a seat and prepared herself for the worst. That day God answered her prayers. Her boss informed her that with the successful completion of her training she was been promoted to relocate to a different store in another state. Ariel smiled peacefully knowing this was her way to escape her abusive relationship with the Muslim without a fight. Within a week she showered him with love beyond measures. But the Friday morning after he left for work within minutes the moving truck came. Ariel was able to pack her belongings to begin her new life. Before they put the last box on the truck Ariel sat down and wrote her final but most touching letter.

Dear My Love,

It has been three loving but challenging years we have had the opportunity to share. When you find this letter I will be gone and starting a new chapter in my life. I loved you beyond measures but I could not allow you to break my spirit any longer. I do not regret the loving and precious moments we spent together, but I must move on. We are not meant to be an item anymore nor can we make it as just friends.

This is the hardest thing I have ever had to do, letting go of love and being loved. Our love was dangerous for each other and it hurts deeply to never be your friend or a part of your life. I pray that God can provide you with the peace you need to replace me in your heart.

Please do not look for me but just let me go and make peace with myself and God. Take the good times and cherish them to make you smile when you are down. Learn from the bad times and allow them to reveal what not to do with your future lady.

We are no longer good for each other mentally or physically. I will continue to pray for you and your soul.

Love,
Ariel

Ariel placed the letter on the kitchen table and put the key to the house on top. She took her last walk through the house to say good bye to the good and bad times. With one lonely tear rolling down her face she walked through the front door, closed it behind herself, kissed her fingertips and placed the final kiss on the closed front door. She walked away to return to the violent love no more.

Happiness

How do you define happiness?
Is it when you find someone to spend the rest of your
life with?
Or is it the day you first fall in love?
Can it be touched, felt, seen, or even tasted?
No. Happiness is when you fall in love with yourself
and who you are as a person.
Happiness starts within and is brought out through
actions and experiences.
You conquer happiness when you forgive those that
despitefully abuse you.
Happiness is when you can smile pass your pain and
love beyond your hurt.
Happiness cannot be given to or taken from you.
You must seek and embrace it through change and
endurance.
Happiness is while facing challenges throughout the
day you remain optimistic,
By capturing and savoring the positive aspect of that day.
Happiness makes you work hard at treating
everyone, especially your enemies, right
The only way to achieve it you must believe in it as
Happiness believes in you!

Shameka J. Walker

Chapter Six

My Best Friend: Featuring Tina

Their agreement was, "When I call, you come but leave your heart at the

door." Both stood their ground and agreed that this was the best thing at

the time for their life and career.

TINA WAS HEADED TO THE AIRPORT to pick up her girlfriend Victoria. She was on vacation and three years had passed since they had last seen each other. Tina arrived at the airport, helped her friend with her bags, and drove straight to the grocery store. Tina knew she had no food at home, which was to be expected from a single woman.

At the grocery store Tina was carefully examining all the fresh fruits when a 6'9" basketball player caught her eye. Standing only 5'1", she began to strategize how to get his attention without making a fool of herself. Her plan was to pretend that she was still shopping, while making sure she could observe him whenever he headed for the checkout counter. Her observations soon paid off. She noticed him in Aisle Two moving toward the checkout stand with only a few items in his cart. Pushing her shopping cart closely behind him, Tina greeted him boldly, "Hello. Can I have your seven digits?"

He smiled at her inquiry with obvious pleasure, and answered, "I have never had anyone so beautiful and fearless ask me for my number. I don't know you but I have no problem taking your number."

Tina reached into her purse, pulled out a pad and pen, wrote down her number and handed him the slip of paper. Victoria observed the entire exchange and admired her friend's courage. "That is my girl and she still got it!"

One month passed before Tina received the first phone call from her grocery store friend. She had almost forgotten that she had given him her number. He quickly reminded her that he was the tall man from the grocery store who had admired her courage. With a smile longer than the Nile River on each of their faces, they talked. They talked nearly every day for the next few weeks.

He was a very urbane man. The women in the local community found him quite charming. Tina was an A-student, excelling in her studies. Neither was looking for commitment; only companionship. Tina had recently left an abusive relationship and her grocery store friend was newly divorced. In order to pursue the obvious interest they had in each other, they created an agreement, "When I call, you come but leave your heart at the door." Tina and her friend stood their ground and agreed that it was the best thing for their lives and careers.

After a twelve hour work shift Tina wanted to go home and relax. As she drove home memories of the many phone conversations with her friend crossed her mind. Being exhausted from work she decided that she would not call him until the following day. She was ecstatic about the friendship she had developed with her new friend. They had been through bad breakups and were searching only to be understood and appreciated.

While Tina headed home to relax her tense body, her friend was baffled that she hadn't called him all day. He watched television as he held the remote in one hand and the cordless phone in the other. He was convinced that Tina would call before the end of the night.

At her place, Tina filled the tub with warm water and warm vanilla bubble bath. She created a peaceful atmosphere by lighting every candle throughout her cozy apartment. Before she stepped into her bath she turned on her favorite jazz compact disc. Tina caressed every inch of her body.

Meanwhile, her friend became very anxious and worried about not hearing from her. To ease his mind he grabbed his car keys and drove straight to Tina's apartment. When he arrived he could hear the music playing and smell the warm, enticing vanilla fragrance coming from her apartment. He knocked several times but his knocks went unanswered. Tina was so engaged in her soothing bath that she did not hear the anxious knock at the door.

Ten minutes passed before he decided to call Tina on his cell phone. Tina heard the call but was unable to answer before the call went to voicemail. After her soothing bath, Tina was startled by a knock at the door. Wrapped in only a towel and dripping water from head to toe she looked through the peek hole. On the other side of the door, her friend was standing with a concerned look on his face. As Tina opened the door he immediately embraced her and planted a sweet, tender kiss on her forehead that made her weak at the knees.

With her right hand on his chest she asked, "Is everything okay?"

He confessed that not hearing from her made him understand how precious and dear their friendship had become. He discovered it was an essential part of his daily routine.

Wanting to be bashful she could not resist the feeling of complete appreciation from her new love. He cherished their friendship but could no longer deny himself of Tina's soft and gentle touch. Being overwhelmed with passion Tina dropped the towel and for the first time in six months their bodies became one.

The grocery store friend found himself mesmerized by Tina, wanting only the best for her. He nurtured her like a newborn baby and wanted to protect her from life's daily challenges.

Tina knew their love was rare and priceless. Because they did not desire a committed relationship, laying down rules in the beginning enabled them to develop a lasting friendship. But they had needs and were willing to commit to one another sexually.

They had a difficult time keeping quiet. The room was better off having no walls because the neighbors felt as though they were part of the romance. He screamed louder than Tina and moved faster than Tina. He had no problem letting the world know that he had met his match and was at Tina's mercy. There love was so strong that he requested Tina be available everyday for the next 30 days. Those 30 days were filled with sleepless nights, climbing walls, falling from the bed, and many memories to keep for a lifetime.

Tina learned the reason he was skeptical about their relationship developing beyond friends. In his prior marriage he had placed his dreams aside for love and family. His divorce opened the door to new opportunities that could satisfy his craving for his own business. Tina did not want him to feel that he could not reach his goal of becoming a business owner. Therefore, she became his best friend and greatest supporter.

Openness and communication about their expectations allowed them to exhibit the true meaning of friendship to everyone that knew them. When they were together everyone knew. It intrigued Tina that even though they did not consider themselves in a relationship he was quick to introduce her to his closest male friends.

Six months later they were still able to encourage and motivate with confidence. He truly treasured Tina as someone he could trust with his deepest fears and insecurities. With that in mind, he was not willing to risk falling in love through a committed relationship and ruin their eccentric companionship. But he was devoted to protecting her ideas as Tina had shielded his goals. Later, they both were able to find true love but learned through their friendship to be their mates' friend, companion, and then lover.

Speechless

Speechless I have never been in my life,
Until I met you and learned to embrace change
Only a select few will ever experience such a joy
Filled with peace, happiness and everlasting love
Sharing secrets, past hurts and future goals
are now second nature
With endless conversation you have opened
my eyes to the purity of having a true friend,
No one but GOD has ever had
such an effect on my life.
Without any hugs or kisses but just spending
quality time together.
I can honestly say you have saved and helped me.
Some would say we are weird or even in denial,
But we will simply call it a beautiful understanding.

Shameka J. Walker

Chapter Seven

My Mentor: Featuring Jasmine

Jasmine explained to her friend that she would love to get away for the

holiday and wanted to.

JASMINE, IN DESPERATE NEED of a vacation, called an old friend. A lot was going on: she was suffering from a bad day at work, being dumped by the man she loved, and no family in town to celebrate Thanksgiving.

After leaving several messages on her friend's answer machine, her phone calls were returned the Sunday before Thanksgiving. Jasmine explained to her friend that she needed a vacation and she would love to get away for the holiday. She asked him if he had any plans. Stunned but happy to hear from her, he asked her to accompany him to New Jersey. Jasmine was so excited that she hung up the phone and immediately started packing before giving him an answer. Before she realized what she had done the phone rang again. "Hello?" she answered.

Shall I take that as a yes?" Jasmine's friend laughingly asked.

Jasmine apologized, laughed, and said, "Without a doubt, yes!"

Their vacation started on a Wednesday. They laughed and talked about any and everything during the six hour trip to their destination. Jasmine knew deep in her heart that this was going to be her best holiday in a long time. Knowing that her friend wanted to be her everything it worried her that he would attempt to take their friendship to a different level. The idea of the next level made her conscious of how she presented herself throughout their trip. The only thing that made her hesitant about being his leading lady was that he was a well known State politician, television host, and business man twenty-four years her senior.

Because she was very gentle, sweet, and loving she would not be able to live with herself if her age was the reason for the end of his successful career. The weekend approached and two nights passed before Jasmine made the mistake of looking into his eyes. The innocent love his eyes expressed along with his good deed of wining and dining her made Jasmine feel obligated to share her body, mind and soul.

Later that night, as he slept, she surprised him by climbing on top and saying quietly, "Just enjoy the ride." To Jasmine's amazement he was already in the position to accept her proposal. For the next hour she turned innocence into something as beautiful as the sunset on a clear day.

Even though Jasmine recognized she could never fulfill all of his heart's desire, she was honored to satisfy all his current needs. Unsure if she would be able to close the door, she made him feel like the happiest man alive. As the moment came to an end, he whispered softly in

Jasmine's ear, "My life will never be the same until I make you my wife. And if that takes a lifetime than you are worth the wait."

Jasmine feared this would happen but was trapped in the moment. Even as she emotionally and physically pulled away he continued to shower her with his true feelings. In return, Jasmine became apprehensive about prolonging their time alone. She asked to go dancing in the city. He was excited about continuing their night and stated that he knew of a night club across the bridge in New York City.

Jasmine immediately got in the shower where she washed away the smell of his cologne and allowed her mind to run free. She did not want to ruin their time together nor did she want to deceive him into thinking she was ready for the next phase of his life. She was having a difficult time with their age gap and career differences.

When she walked out of the shower, he was waiting for her. He sat expectantly on the edge of the bed waiting to see his princess. Unable to hide his feelings, he reached out and embraced Jasmine. She quickly turned her face as he attempted to kiss her lips and urged him to move forward for their evening social event.

Looking elegant in a long strapless black gown with silver rhinestones, Jasmine walked gracefully to the car. As he opened the car door he spoke softly, "You look amazing and your beauty is priceless."

Turning, Jasmine acknowledged his compliment, "Thank you." Her reply was soft and contrite.

During the short ride to New York, he played music that enforced his desires. She had to endure the luxury of being treated like a princess as her face disguised her deepest fears. Jasmine was troubled about being loved, in spite of her flaws, while he risked everything for love.

At the club, Jasmine danced with everyone but her date. It was her attempt to buy time to help him understand that she was not what he needed. He stood back while drinking a glass of water and admired her beauty. What Jasmine failed to comprehend was that she was only giving him extra time to understand the love they shared. He was not a jealous man, accepting everything about her including her age. He was proud that everyone found his leading lady attractive enough to ask her to dance. At the end of the night he knew she would be going home with him and was happy that she was having a good time. Before the club closed, he walked over to Jasmine and requested the final dance. Jasmine's friend lovingly held her tight; she laid her head on his chest. As she listened to their hearts beat together he whispered in her ear, "I will not pressure you into loving me as I love you. It is okay that you are not ready to travel life's journey with me, but it will never stop me from loving you. I appreciate you looking out for my career instead of being blinded by love."

It seemed as though the song continued through the night. They left the club with a passionate understanding of their love and the willingness to accept the fact that age does matter when it comes to maturing in love.

Chapter Eight

My Chat Line Flirt: Featuring Regina

"Regina knew she had to have privacy for what was about to take place.

The master bedroom closet became the perfect choice."

REGINA LAY IN THE BED unable to sleep when she saw the number to meet local singles flash across the television screen. The number had appeared several times throughout the night before she noticed it. After second thoughts, Regina finally decided to write the number down and call to see whom she might meet. Being sexually frustrated made it very easy for her to pick up the phone and dial the number. Even though she was not sure what she was getting herself into, Regina found the whole idea intriguing. She was looking for someone to talk to until she fell asleep. To her surprise she made a connection with someone that shared her same interests.

He seemed to be a very respectful and nice person with an outgoing personality. After getting to know a little about each other, they wanted to take their conversation to the next level. Regina confessed that she was sexually in need and looking for someone to assist her in climaxing over the phone so she could fall asleep.

Her friend confirmed that he was up for the challenge. Because she had company in her home Regina sought for privacy in the master bedroom walk-in closet.

She positioned herself on the floor wearing only the fragrances from her earlier shower. She lay back to relax and imagined herself on an island with only her present lover. Her friend began to set the mood for a short but enchanting romance that would end with fireworks.

He started by telling Regina that he had undressed her with his teeth. He was now caressing her body with his tongue. As he massaged her breast with his lips, he began to enter her. He was stunned that she was so wet and he was able to just slip inside her as though it was familiar territory.

Regina moaned with a sigh of relief from a week of built-up pressure. Her moans of delight were so sensational that he felt as though he was in the closet with her and Regina was being satisfied in every way possible. Regina, reaching her peak, cried out, "I'm coming! I'm coming! I'm coming!"

Then she exhaled and informed her friend his services were greatly appreciated and to have a good night. As she began to hang up the phone he cried out, "Don't go!" Hearing the plea in his voice, Regina made the hasty decision not to hang up. Instead, holding the phone to her ear, she asked, "Was there something else you needed to say?" He became very inquisitive and confessed that he found her extremely fascinating.

Regina did not intend to continue the conversation with her new friend. After her orgasmic experience she just craved sleep. He requested her telephone number in order to talk privately with her in the future and to get off the expensive chat line. Even though her mind was filled with doubt she took his number and stated she would call him in a minute. Regina returned his call without evaluating the consequences. Unfortunately, after an hour of intense seductive conversation she went to sleep while lying on the phone. He called her name over and over but when Regina didn't answer he hung up.

The next day, Regina called him to apologize. She asked how she could make it up to him. Without delay he asked her to accompany him to dinner. Regina agreed to dinner with the stipulations that she pick the time and the place. He replied, "You have a deal."

Later that night they met at her favorite restaurant where the menu is filled with seafood and vegetables. Feeling a little uncomfortable she invaded his privacy by asking essential questions concerning his past and current life. He was so captivated by her vivacious body and vigorous personality that her questions went unanswered. Quickly coming back to reality he expressed to her that he was seeking his soul mate but wanted first to develop a friendship.

Regina informed him that she had no desire to date at this time. As they were leaving the restaurant she thanked him for dinner but informed him that she would rather they not see each other again. Regina found it necessary to educate him that she was lonely the night she called the chat line and not searching for love.

She was at a point in her life where she was learning to fall in love and learning to love herself first. Without prolonging the inevitable Regina politely excused herself from the table, shook his hand, and left him to pay the bill. They never spoke to or saw each other again.

Chapter Nine

My Dream Love Affair: Featuring Georgina

While the music played, he whispered in her ear as he held her, "Are you

sure you want to walk through this door never to return?"

THERE WAS TROUBLE BREWING in paradise. Even though Georgina had it all she lived the ideal dream lifestyle of a cherished, married woman. She had the perfect gentleman for a husband, two beautiful kids, a mansion on the hill and enough money to never be in need. She was considered by her peers to be one of the most intelligent, independent, and outgoing people you could ever meet. Her mind was filled with ideas and her talents were unlimited. She was able to wear several hats and climb any mountain to succeed in any venture. Many in the community depended on her for emotional, spiritual and physical support.

Yet, while trying to keep it together on the outside she was dying on the inside. She had been successful at hiding her pain better than the Secret Service hid an eyewitness. Even though she was loved by numerous people, Georgina struggled to fulfill her heart's desire. At this point in her life, that something special had eluded her.

As Georgina rested her head on the pillow she fell into a deep dream. In the dream a friend introduced her to an amazing man. It was a meeting of the mind and the soul. She and this amazing man called each other on a regular basis. After several telephone calls, it became apparent to them that something electric connected them. All he craved was to learn as much as possible about the jewel on the other end of the telephone. It was a rainy night when they decided to meet. They were greatly impressed with each other. Her beauty was as radiant and inviting as sunshine to the man. He was instantly mesmerized by the purity of her personality and the wonder of her character. His physical stature was eye boggling to the woman. He stood 6'1", with broad shoulders, a small waistline and narrow hips. His stance was that of a man comfortable with himself. His dark brown eyes seem to hold mysteries that intrigued her and seemed to invite her in.

Thoughts of her family were in the back of her mind, but she felt a strong physical urge to fulfill her deepest desires with her new love. She wanted to discover the mystery in his eyes. Affected by the powerfully charged atmosphere, Georgina asked if she could spend the night.

He was hesitant to agree, but he could not refuse her because she sincerely intrigued him. Georgina sat down, removed her shoes and made herself at home. While she sat on the couch and watched Law & Order he prepared a salad for them in his modern, well-stocked kitchen. The girl could hardly believe she was in the home of the man that could very likely complete her.

She blocked out all her troubling thoughts deciding to turn the moment into one to remember. After they completed their meal and everything had been put away, he turned off the television and turned on the stereo. Soft, romantic music began to float in from every direction of the room encompassing her in its melody and compelling lyrics. While the music played, he whispered in her ear as he held her, "Are you sure you want to walk through this door never to return?"

Without hesitation, she responded with a smile as pure as gold and nodded her head, "Yes."

Shortly after agreeing to be loved by the man, she began to move to the music. Slowly, methodically, and provocatively she undressed herself. He laid back on the couch and enjoyed the rousing show being performed for his eyes only. When there was not a stitch of clothing left on her vivacious body, she moved toward him and caressed his masculine skin with her soft skin. The man lay with his eyes closed; waiting for what he knew would be the experience of a lifetime. He did not have long to wait. Soon, the hot, moist tongue of his love moved along his magnificent dark toned body. Up and down she went careful to cover every inch. Her lips fell upon a soft rock that needed more attention than any other part of his body. As she caressed his rock, he confirmed that she had captured his heart by the cracking of his toes. He could not believe that a stranger, in such a short time, had become his everything. He was in love.

With great effort, the man stood up, taking his new love - his queen, by the hand. He led her upstairs and invited her to finish their enchanted romance in the palace he had never shared with another woman. She had inherited the key to his heart which had been locked away for several years.

Now it was his turn. He began to show her what pure love felt like. Lovingly, he kissed each of her breasts, circling his tongue and focusing upon the central point until she thought she would burst from her skin. All the while, his hands played in the area no one could view bringing her to a new level of ecstasy she never imagined. Without protecting themselves and with no regard of bringing forth new life he entered her and firmly began to rock her world. They came together with a resounding, heartfelt crash. The room was lifted from its foundation to another planet. On that planet they were able to live as one and erase any worries from their minds. They savored every second, knowing it would end one day.

The man was everything she had ever desired. He was able to take control of her mind and show her a love unknown. Georgina knew the fire they ignited would never stop burning and would always remain alive. No one could ever begin to understand what was shared or felt for he had revealed a love inside her she was unaware of until the day she walked into his life.

Completely satisfied and feeling the heat of the sunrise on her face, Georgina yawned lazily, slowly opened her dreamy eyes, glanced over, and said, "Good morning my darling husband, you were wonderful. Was the night as magical for you too?"

Loving You

Loving you has been so easy,

One look into your eyes forced my heart to

melt and skip a beat.

All doubts was shattered while dreams began to

come true.

I smile daily thinking about the love you have

given me.

How suddenly you are part of my everyday

decisions.

Without your gentle touch

and soft spoken words,

My day can never be complete.

You are the reason for my smiles, laughter, and

tears of joy.

One call from you erases every negative

thought and situation,

Regardless of the topic of conversation

I conquer every ounce of your attention

Since loving you has been so easy,

I accept you as you are and wouldn't have you

any other way.

Shameka J. Walker

Chapter Ten 10

My Loving Husband: Featuring Samantha

"Samantha had searched for love in all the wrong places and just when she had thrown in the towel, he found her. And now, today was her day."

SAMANTHA HAD WAITED all her life to be found by her soul mate that would love her unconditionally. In less than three hours she would be married and thought it would be an easy task to let her guard down and allow the man of her dreams to shower her with pure love. She had searched for love in all the wrong places and, just when she had made up her mind to throw in the towel love found her.

At sunset, on Valentine's Day, she walked down the long aisle to confess her eternal devotion to a man she had met only seven weeks earlier. As she took her final stroll of singularity all her attention focused on the tall, dark, and handsome man dressed in Navy winter white waiting at the altar. Standing face to face they were able to feel the warmth of each other eyes and see the sincerity of their love within their smiles. As he touched Samantha's face he began to confess to her that she was the woman that completed him and mesmerized him to the point that he could never dream of getting old.

Samantha knew it was no fault of her own that this man came into her life. Only God could answer the question heavily on her mind, *How and why did God bless and enrich my life with such a wonderful man?* She realized that some things are not to be understood but accepted. As the Bishop pronounced them man and wife their lips touched to signify the beginning of a lifetime of true love.

Now, seven weeks after marriage they found themselves at a couple's retreat sponsored by their church. Even though they were in the beginning stage of their marriage they were excited about the retreat. Samantha felt the retreat would likely uncover the unwanted baggage they had brought into their marriage. They both were fully aware that marriage was more than they both imagined or bargained for; but at the same time, they knew it was ordained by God.

Before the open night of meet and greet they made each other a promise to be open-minded; open to what the instructors and other couples had to share concerning how they made their marriage work.

To their surprise their relationship made an immaculate turn for the better during the powerful and fulfilling weekend. During the retreat they were taught the importance of open communication within a marriage. Samantha and her husband were not new to the game but new to each other. After many broken promises and hurts from their past relationships they pledged to always listen to each others problems and share each other's dreams.

Saturday night of the retreat, as they returned to their hotel suite, their relationship had reached another level that would normally take twenty years of trial and error to accomplish. They were instructed, as the many other couples, to return to their hotel suite and with listening ears release all past hurts, pains, failures and disappointments without judging but supporting.

That night they were able to liberate anything and everyone that blocked the growth of their love and vowed to take notice of what satisfy and made each other whole. Not until after Samantha and her husband genuine but enchanted confession were they able to exchange the keys to each other's hearts. At that very moment, the night became magical as the sky filled with fireworks.

He was overwhelmed with so much passion that he effortlessly lifted Samantha off her feet and laid her on the king size bed completely covered with their wedding colors of white, red, and pink roses. He became lost to the point of no return and craved to share all of himself with his beloved wife, Samantha. As he kissed her luscious lips, tears began to flow from her eyes. But he swiftly moved his lips to her cheek to capture the tears signifying his level of dedication and devotion to only bring her joy, peace, pleasure and eternal happiness. In the mist of their lives becoming one, their love reached the pinnacle of its affection when he brought Samantha to her first orgasmic experience. Samantha was able to finally release years of pain, suffering, hurt and hate when she softly cried out, "I love you with all that is inside me and I promise to be true to myself and you for a lifetime!" As he made love to her until sunrise it was at that very moment Samantha became his virtuous woman. God had confirmed he was her soul mate to share everyday of the rest of their lives together with integrity, honesty, and pure Godly love.

Chapter 11

My Soul Mate Featuring Jaleen

JALEEN KISSED HER GIRLS GOOD-BYE as she boarded Flight 517 to Jamaica for a much needed vacation. The time had finally come for her to take advantage of the trip she won six months earlier. This is the first vacation she had taken since her fifteen-year marriage ended almost a year ago. As she boarded the plane tears began to stream down her face. Not able to see through the tears, she passed her assigned seat. The gentleman in row 25 noticed that Jaleen seemed to be distracted and offered her a helping-hand. She quickly rejected his help and then turned around to find her seat in row 15.

Jaleen's heart ached and she felt overwhelmed being a single parent due to a failed marriage. Hopeless and abandoned, she yearned for more for her girls and for herself. She wanted love but did not know how to let go of all of the pain that consumed her.

After her flight, Jaleen took a shuttle to the luxury hotel where a Penthouse Suite was reserved for her enjoyment. Absolutely amazed at the beauty of the island and its beautiful beaches, she decided to enjoy the time away as she took it all in from the hotel's glass elevator. She unpacked, changed into her bathing suit, and headed downstairs to catch some sun on the beach.

Jaleen barely noticed the young man who entered the elevator on the tenth floor as she looked dreamily at the clear blue ocean water. Without saying a word, they road to the first floor and then went their separate ways. Even though she did not notice or recognize him he remembered her from the plane and turned for a second glance. He watched Jaleen as she walked towards the beach.

Jaleen found a great view on the beach, ordered the house drink, and watched the waves go back and forth. While relaxing, she drifted off asleep without a care in the world. At nightfall, she was in the same spot sleeping peacefully.

The man from the plane saw this as an opportunity to wake her and introduce himself. He touched her face with his gentle hands and asked, "Ma'am are you ok?"

His voice and touch startled her to consciousness, "Where am I?" Panic was visible in her eyes.

"You've been sleeping here for hours," the young man explained as Jaleen gathered her things. He gently tugged her arm as she proceeded to walk away. "Please don't rush off. Everything is alright."

Taken back by his beautiful accent and kindness, Jaleen stopped, laughed, and thanked him for all his help.

"Your beauty is as radiant as sunshine," the man explained, "I noticed you on the airplane and could not get you out of my mind. I wanted to talk to you but you rejected me so I didn't know how to approach you again."

"I'm so sorry for my behavior," she said, thinking *I had to be out of my mind to not be cordial with you.* "I had a lot on my mind earlier. It's no excuse."

After talking for a few moments, she hesitantly agreed to have dinner with him later that night.

Jaleen returned to her suite with great anticipation of the night to come. She smiled brightly—inside and out. Jaleen took a long hot shower, put on her favorite fragrance, and found an appropriately sexy outfit: a strapless short black dress and three inch black heels. She completed her look with pearl stud earrings and a matching necklace. Satisfied with her appearance, Jaleen grabbed her purse and headed for the rooftop for dinner.

The tall, caramel skin-toned man from the beach stood next to a table for two, decorated with black and white linens and a beautiful centerpiece made of yellow roses. Impressed with the effort he put into the date, she walked over to the table and graciously accepted the kiss he planted on her cheek.

Tall, dark, handsome and chivalrous she thought as she sat in the chair he pulled out for her. Over the course of the evening his presence overwhelmed her, not because he was every bit of six foot four inches tall but because he made her feel like time had stood still for her to be free from the pain. The food, ambiance, and company were great.

A few hours before sunrise, he walked her back to her suite. When Jaleen invited him in for tea he declined. "I prefer to keep the evening perfect," he said and kissed Jaleen on the forehead to bid her goodnight.

Early the next morning she was awakened by a doorbell. Not expecting company, she grabbed one of the thick bath robes and went to the door. To her surprise, she was greeted by a concierge with a portable table filled with breakfast pastries. A long yellow rose similar to the ones from last night was stapled to a card that read:

To a special someone who has taken my breath away.

She looked at the man who brought her the food. His expression was dumbfounded when she asked who sent it. Jaleen gave him a tip and the young man walked away.

"I promised to never leave you or forsake you. I have heard your prayers," she heard a voice whisper. All at once, the words seem to be close and far away. Jaleen didn't know how to take her situation. The man from the night before was evasive and now she was hearing voices. Still doubting everything, she tried to be optimistic and positive but the pain slowly began to ache in her heart. It wasn't heavy as it was before but present nonetheless.

Later that day she received a call from the front desk. The voice on the other end informed her that her car had arrived. Knowing that she do not have a car, Jaleen attempted to explain that there was a mistake. But the receptionist insisted that the car was for Jaleen.

Wearing a long sundress and sandals, Jaleen went to the lobby and the concierge from breakfast pointed her to a black stretch limo. When the door opened, her date from the night before got out, kissed her on the cheek and helped her into the car.

After a forty minute drive they arrived at a beautiful mansion overlooking the countryside. Speechless, she followed the man into the oversized home. After touring the magnificent dwelling, Jaleen asked, "Why are we here?"

He stopped grabbed both of her hands, "I own the hotel where you're staying and I've been searching for a wife for more than three years. I've faithfully prayed for God to place my wife on my path so that I could find her." He paused and examined Jaleen's expression. "I hope that I'm not being to forward but from the moment I laid eyes on you I knew you were the one."

Standing there frozen and speechless, Jaleen felt weak in the knees but he caught her in his strong arms before she fell to the ground. The voice from breakfast confirmed in her heart the words of the man who was holding her, protecting her. God let her know that she was being rewarded for her faithfulness.

Her mind raced about her daughters and how her family would accept her being with *this* man. Momentary cloudiness filled her mind when he kissed her deeply and said, "Everything I have is what you have. This," he gestured to the grand mansion on the hill in which they stood, "is yours because it is mine. You won't have to want or wish for anything ever again. Be my wife, please?"

"No," she said, sprinted for the door, jumped into the limo, and requested that the driver take her back to the hotel. She couldn't get the man and what he offered her out of her mind. When Jaleen arrived at the hotel she tearfully packed her bags, called the airlines to change her flight, and left in the first taxi she saw. Once again, Jaleen was running away instead of handling the task at hand.

"Jaleen," a voice called to her when she approached the gate at the airport.

Her heart no longer just ached; every part of her ached with pain and throbbed with confusion.

"I'm not letting you go. I've prayed and searched for you to long to allow you to just disappear." He said but clarified his statement, realizing that fear was in Jaleen's eyes. "I'll do whatever it takes for you to be my wife. What can I do?"

"I'm afraid. This is all too perfect, too sudden," Jaleen answered.

"Why would you pray for something but run when God answers your prayer? Give it a chance." He reached over grabbed her suitcase, "Give love a chance."

Jaleen decided to stay and see what was in store for her. The young man continued to adorn her with attention, affection, and love during her stay. He treated her like a lady. By the end of the trip, they were both undeniably in love with each other.

As Jaleen prepared to leave the island, she grew panicked because she could not reach her family. Longing to see her girls but saddened to leave her love, she gathered her things and went to the lobby. When she stepped off the elevator she noticed that the entire first floor of the hotel had been decorated for a wedding. Standing before her were her girls, her family, a few of her friends, and the man of her dreams. After giving her family a long overdue greeting, Jaleen was whisked away to the bridal suite where she was transformed into a beautiful bride.

On the way down the aisle, she thanked God for allowing her a chance of real love with her soul mate. She was finally able to live and love beyond her pain. Jaleen no longer took for granted that her pain would test and make her strong to be truly prepared for all that God had in store for her. This time the tears that filled her eyes were a result of pure joy as she walked towards the man of her dreams.

Chapter 12

My Secret Lover: Featuring Marisa

MARISA HAD TWENTY MINUTES before her shift started and she was running late. Going eighty-five miles per hour with a one track mind she failed to see the State trooper hiding in a near distance on the right. As she focused on getting to work, the cruiser pulled out behind her and flashed bright blue lights. *Now, I'm really gonna be late* she thought as she slowly pulled over praying the officer was in an understanding mood.

"I'm so sorry," she apologized as he approached. "I'm running late for a speaking engagement and didn't realize I was speeding."

"I'm feeling kind of generous today," the officer said. "Since it's not busy on the roads today, I'm gonna give you a warning but you have to promise to slow down."

Relieved, Marisa smiled, thanked the officer and proceeded to work. With only a few minutes to spare, she arrived safely and was able to deliver her speech flawlessly.

Shortly after her meeting Marisa received a phone call from her best friend Queen. Queen was in town and wanted to meet her for lunch to discuss her many relationship issues. Queen's standards for the perfect man were so high that all her past relationships only lasted a few weeks. She describes everyone she dated as *The One*. Marisa agreed to meet her for lunch at their favorite restaurant downtown. Marisa swiftly finished some last minute paperwork, logged off her computer, and walked to the restaurant.

Arriving ten minutes early, Marisa decided to order herself a virgin Piña colada, very thick with no cream. As she waited for her chronically late friend, she noticed the officer from the traffic stop. She watched him scope out the restaurant. When their eyes locked, Marisa looked away quickly. Seeing him made her uncomfortable but she had to suck it up as the waitress seated him at the table directly across from hers.

The closer he got the more nervous she became. She wondered if he might have changed his mind about giving her a ticket.

Ten minutes passed and still no sign of Queen. Marisa, looking down at her watch, was startle by a firm voice asking, "Are you waiting on someone?"

She looked up and it was the officer speaking. Marisa responded, "Yes my forever fashionable late best friend." Moments later she received a text message from Queen. As usual something had *come up* and she needed to reschedule. Disappointed, she sighed, "Well change of plans I am not expecting anyone."

"Well, you can have lunch with me," he offered.

Marisa blushed. "I'm a married woman and do not think that would be a good idea."

"I'm an officer of the law," he stuck out his chest teasingly. "I promise you and your marriage will be safe in my company."

Knowing she should have given a swift *no*, Marisa had lunch with him. They ordered chicken Alfredo with broccoli. While eating lunch they learned that they had more in common than a love for chicken Alfredo.

In an effort not to mislead the officer Marisa spoke repeatedly about Queen. The officer seemed more interested in her than her friend. After dinner, Marisa innocently handed the officer her business card when he asked if they could exchange numbers. As she excused herself from the table she thanked the officer for his generosity and for the great conversation. When she reached for her meal ticket the officer stated, "Don't worry lunch is on me." She thanked him again and exited back to work.

After work Marisa received a call from Queen apologizing for missing lunch and promising to make it up to her the next time she is in town. Even though Marisa talks to Queen on a regular basis she travels a lot with her job and only comes home three to four times a year. They have a sisterly bond to the point that they are able to finish each other sentences. Queen stated that she wanted to let her know that she has once again broken up with the guy that she thought was *The One*. After a long drawn out discussion Marisa learned that the only reason Queen broke off the relationship with her most recent boy friend was because the gentleman worked 50 - 60 hours a week and he always had an excuse of why he could not travel. To her surprise he also hid the fact that he has three children from two previous relationships and half of his check was being taken for child support. Queen failed to get the gentlemen complete explanation before making the hasty decision to end the relationship.

Three months passed before the officer decided to call Marisa at work. Marisa excitingly answered the call which lasted for forty-five minutes. A large part of their conversation consisted of the many failed infertility treatments she had experienced with her husband over the past six years of marriage. Marisa considered herself strong willed and full of faith but at that very moment she was overwhelmed with doubt and felt like a failure. The officer allowed her to talk without interruption and was sympathetic to her current situations. As she was speaking with the officer the secretary handed her a message from Queen requesting that she call her at her earliest convenient. That note changed her conversation with the officer to discuss her girl friends many problems. The officer offered her some good advice to give to her friend prior to ending their call. She returned Queen's call but it went straight to voicemail.

Shortly after many phone calls to her job Marisa, feeling mentally frustrated, decided to meet the officer at his home on the west side of town. She only worked until noon that day and was invited to his home for lunch. While there they laughed and talked about her marriage, their struggle to get pregnant, and of course her friend Queen. She had finally found someone of the opposite sex that she could talk to freely without being judged but someone who actually took the time to listen and allowed her to talk for hours. Marisa had a great provider as a husband that loved her dearly but he had shut down due to her inability to get pregnant. He loved her but his desire to have a child made him feel less than a man after trying so many years and three miscarriages. This caused him to feel punished verses blessed and for the past few weeks there has been very little communication between the two.

Three hours past without notice from Marisa or the officer. Marisa started to cry while discussing that her husband had moved into the guess room stating that he needs time alone to figure out his feelings and the direction of their marriage. The officer could not just stand back and watch her cry so he pulled her close why holding her tight to assure her that he was there for her. The officer consoled Marisa and allowed her to cry out to free her pains. As he wiped her tears their lips touched which sparked the beginning of an intense nine months affair.

Throughout those nine months they made an agreement to not fall in love but simply to enjoy the moment to free inner frustrations. Together they explored the path of a married couple through adultery and a first class ticket to hell. Marisa had no plans to end her marriage but was willing to find the one thing worth fighting for to rekindle the fire she once shared with her husband.

The officer worked hard to say the right things, intrigue her her mind and caress her body like no other even though he knew the relationship had no future. But one mistake was made. No matter how hard he tried he found himself developing feelings for Marisa. His worst fear came to life when he confessed to Marisa that he wanted her to end her marriage and begin a new chapter as his wife. Feeling that the officer had shattered their agreement she explained to him that she will do whatever it took to save her marriage even if it included ending their affair. The officer strongly felt betrayed and used by Marisa and was not willing to just let her go. After several unanswered phone calls he realized that Marisa was serious about saving her marriage.

Marisa turned her back on the officer and worked overtime to make her husband love her again. From time to time she would have a distant memory of the officer but felt secure in her decision to end the affair. Marisa and her husband decided to seek counseling and after seven weeks of marriage classes from their pastor with other couples suffering from infertility they came to the conclusion that their love were stronger than any problems or challenges that comes their way.

It had been several months since she had heard from her best friend Queen so she was very excited when her secretary transferred the call. Marisa quickly answered and asked her where she has been? Queen informed her that she has been very busy with work and her new boo. Marisa was shocked that she was just hearing the first of Queen dating again with her calling to discuss every single detail of their relationship. She stated that this relationship is different than all the others and she would be in town in two weeks and wanted to meet Marisa and her husband for lunch at the restaurant downtown. Queen assured her that she will not cancel this time and that she had some fascinating news to share with them.

Two weeks passed and Marisa and her husband were patiently waiting on Queen's arrival at the restaurant. Marisa was enjoying the time with her husband gazing into each other eyes and feeling overwhelmed with falling back in love with each other. Suddenly Queen comes through the doors with a smile larger than gold. Instantly Marisa noticed she looked different and had a beautiful glow. They all greeted each other with long hugs and friendly kisses. As they were taking their seats Queen announced she has traveled with her new boo and wanted them to be the first to meet him but he was parking the car.

Minutes later the officer walked through the door and Queen waived him to where they were seated. Queen introduced the officer not just has her new boo but as her husband of two months. They had eloped in Vegas. Without hesitation she proceed to tell them that they were now six weeks pregnant and want Marisa and her husband to be the baby's God parents. Marisa face became white as snow but she controlled her composure while hiding behind her smile, without response of anger,

because it would expose her too.

Questions & Answers

If you could change one thing about your past what would that be and why?

I would change the fact that I waited until age 14 to tell an adult about the abuse that had been taking place for the past 10 years. Maybe if the adults in my life knew about the pain I had to endure alone, I could have received the help I needed. I don't believe I would have allowed myself to be in abusive relationships in my young adult years.

What is your inspiration for the short stories?

They were inspired by various relationships. Women who have been abused mentally, sexually, physically and emotionally found themselves while searching for Mr. Right.

How did you develop each character?

Each character was inspired by someone from my past directly or indirectly. I learned at a young age that people come in your life for a season and some for a lifetime. Therefore, I was serious about leaving the negative aspects of past relationships in the past. While being adamant about taking something positive from the experience that in return made me a better person and open to change in the future.

Why do some women have a need to please others before themselves?

As young ladies we are taught to be the peacemaker in relationships. That can include giving and compromising body, mind and soul. But compromising and giving do not mean losing your sense of who you are as a person. We must maintain our individuality and bring class and character to the relationship. It is compelling as women we inspire, motivate, caress, and love ourselves' first, before we can successfully please or even satisfy anyone else.

How do you balance a healthy relationship between work and family?

It is imperative that you understand that work and family or two very important but different responsibilities. I have learned that when I go to work I am there to do the job that I get paid to do. And when I am home that is my sacred time with my family and work has nowhere to sleep in my house.

My Story of Overcoming the Odds

Growing up in a small town in Mississippi I was faced with different trials and experienced some amazing triumphs. My past is filled with ups and downs as well as tears and laughter. I have endured pain that a child should never have to feel or succumb too. Through my pain I was able to understand that love can hurt and love can bring joy. Laughter kept me sane and able to face another day.

At the age of four I was approached by someone, I will call a 'male friend,' whom I trusted that introduced me to the world of pornography. This was his way of gaining control of my mind in order to take advantage of my youthful body. His plan prevailed because, for the next ten years he proceeded to molest me every opportunity that came available. He convinced me that it was a part of growing up to be a beautiful woman.

During those ten years my body became used to being caressed, aroused, and sadly to say, sometimes even satisfied. My hormones were knocked clear out of order. I knew that his hands were designed to protect and shelter me; not abuse and use me. It became very difficult for me to distinguish between love, lust, and abuse. I literally knew when, where, and how each scenario was going to take place.

As I matured I came to the realization that the abuse would never end until I made a stand and told him, "I am not going to be your sex toy for your own gratification while my mind is tormented with nightmares and insecurities about my sexuality."

So, I made it my ultimate goal to never let anyone into my heart and when I loved, the only way I knew how was to love hard. I had two choices: let my past make me or allow it to break me. But I was too determined to be broken. Therefore, I picked up the broken pieces of my heart and vowed to let my life be an example to others. I chose to not give up on love but to be very careful whom I let into my world.

When I found somebody to love I felt obligated to share with them my past. In return, there were times it didn't seem like a good idea because he would start to feel pity instead of love. It was hard to develop a relationship filled with true love because just when I let my guard down he would say, "You are an amazing person but you deserve someone better." If that didn't end the relationship then he felt the need to strike me or destroy my self-esteem. Then there were times when someone I dated had no idea how to articulate how he felt or what he expected out of the relationship.

It wasn't until I met and married my husband that I learned the true meaning of finding love and being loved. My husband is an awesome man of God that preaches about what it means to love and forgive. It was April 2001 in San Diego, CA when I attended a revival about forgiveness when God set me free and opened the door for me to set my abusers free.

Like the words of the late Dr. King sang, "Free at last, Free at last. Thank God Almighty, I'm free at last!"

SHAMEKA WALKER

Made in the USA
Columbia, SC
01 May 2018